ReverSoul of Fortune

Do Not Assume (Lineage)

Redford Branch Library
21200 Grand River
Detroit, MI 48219
313-481-1820

M. H. Goshen

Copyright © 2022 by Marc H. Goshen
All rights reserved.

This book or parts thereof may not be reproduced in any form, stored in retrieval system, or transmitted in any form by any means- electronic, mechanical, photocopy, recording, or otherwise- without prior written permission of the publisher, except as provided by United States of America copyright law.

This is a work of fiction, Names, characters, places and incidents either are products of the author's imagination or are used fictitiously. Any resemblance to actual persons, living or dead is strictly coincidental.

Published by M.H Goshen
Published in association with Amazon KDP
ISBN: 979-8-8487135-6-5
Printed in the United States of America

Creative Credits:
Story concept and developmental contributions by my wife, Mrs. Goshen

Dedicated to:

- *The Most High, Alpha and Omega; my all and everything. Without you none of this exists; with you, impossible is just a word.*
- *My parents and my sister Denise, I love y'all immensely.*
- *My wife, next up for being my all and everything; love you and thank you.*
- *My children, life's short do what you love.*

Table of Contents

Prologue vii

Chapter 1: Fortune 1

Chapter 2: Put Up or Shut Up! 15

Chapter 3: Misfortune 31

Chapter 4: Kindred Encounters 49

Chapter 5: Denial Is Deadly 69

Chapter 6: Looks Are Deceiving 85

Chapter 7: Reconciliation & Redemption 103

Prologue

"KING" of The Hate

"White Supremacy is as real as niggers believing their lives matter!" This wasn't how the PMG's meetings were usually brought to order, but this was something weighing heavy on old King's heart. It was how he felt. Words to live by, spoken by the leader of the PMG (Power Movement Group) Klayton Kincheloe. "King" was what he preferred to be called by all that knew him. Klayton was a New Age racist...wealthy, educated and handsome but with all the fire, hatred and vigor of his predecessors, if not more. Not only was he a proud Virginian but he was especially proud that he was the "chosen one" to lead in the birthplace of slavery. That had to be ordained by God Himself. He didn't believe in coincidences; he never once saw that word in the Holy Bible. He never saw the letters DNA in there either, but he vehemently believed in lineage.

Jesus had to have come from somewhere, even if He was a Jew. In fact, He was introduced in the good book by the telling of His lineage. He was the King of the Jews and Klayton was King of the White man. That's why the bylaws stated that all current and future members of the PMG take a DNA test. It was mandatory to be tested in order to keep the integrity and purity of his beloved organization intact. Any member who declined to take the test would be ostracized. The test was a requirement in the application process for those interested in joining. If your results were found to be contaminated with races other than Caucasian derivatives, with Caucasian not being the dominate race; membership in the PMG would be immediately revoked! Up to and including a lifetime of being excommunicated, fines and willful subjection to racial profiling and subsequent law enforcement harassment periodically. If it's good enough for the Blacks, then it'd be good enough for you too!

The colorful language that opens this story are the words of my great nephew, Klayton Jefferson Kincheloe. I don't need a whole bunch of fuss about who I am. That's not important but I would like ya to be able to follow along and know when I'm talking to ya. Just consider me your friendly raconteur. Nonetheless, this is an odyssey that examines the substance and soul of a man, and at times Klayton questions whether or not he is minus one or the other. None of us are exempt from the judgement of the Creator. Regardless of whichever way you choose to believe. But I'm sure without an ounce of uncertainty, that every breathing soul has, at one time or another made a judgement about an individual which was not spot on. We all do it. I'm guilty of it myself. Though Klayton's grand-daddy and I have the same womb in common, that's about all we share. I sure don't partake in either him or his son's sentiments concerning folk of color.

I'll be talking you through this journey and doing a bit more of it than what I'm used to. But I thought it was imperative to tell you the truth from…let's just call it an unbiased perspective if you will. Old King wouldn't do it no justice. My perspective is slightly different seeing as how I'm speaking to you from the other side of the living. But it has in no way warped my sense of being a good judge of character. Now, now there's no need to get all creeped out just cause the dead guy is telling ya this story. I'm the closest thing to the source; living or dead. You get the picture. Besides, we all gotta go one day. Well, if there's any question of where I'm speaking to you from, I'm in the place where central air comes standard. I don't think they even allow fans in the other place. Now that we've gotten those issues out of the way, let's get on with what we came here for.

CHAPTER 1
Fortune

Klayton Jefferson Kincheloe was born into wealth, and with that came a plethora of privileges. Not the kind that comes with *just* being a white person. Anybody can just be white…well…not anybody. Hell, who'd want to be *just* white anyways? That isn't enough if you want to live life the way it was intended to be lived, regardless of color. You're going to need plenty of capital to cover the expenses that come with living a *privileged* life. And for our family, the Kincheloe family, that would be no problem at 'all!

Being an only child definitely didn't help King learn how to share or sharpen any of his social skills, so he got by without them as best as he could. By the time young Klayton had reached the ripe old age of seven, he was already the owner of a stable of horses, three ATVs, two motor dirt bikes, and 175 acres to enjoy all of them. Eleven years later he was the proud owner of a chain of grocery stores that lined the east coast from Rhode Island to Florida and was looking to expand through the mid-west and beyond. I told his daddy he was making the boy rotten, but he paid me no never mind.

By the time he was eighteen he was worth $58,000,000.00. Not a bad net worth for someone who'd never worked a day in his life. Klayton never used his money to buy people's affection. He couldn't care less about *their feelings*. Hell, he barely had any of his own. He bought people instead. He didn't care about what people thought of him just as long as they were compliant with his demands. He used his money for power and control.

He learned at an early age from his father and grandfather that money was nice to have, but power and control were far better. Pervis and Avril Kincheloe believed that a fool and his money would soon part ways, but even if you *were* poor, you could use your power to manipulate and control people within a system. Why, if you mastered this it wouldn't be long before you were running the system itself! Being poor was just a temporary setback. The money would come, and with more money, more power would surely follow. To them, power took shape in various forms but it all came from God.

Klayton's father and grandfather both believed power came in the form of a voice. Be it a singing voice, a talking voice, or a preaching voice. They knew the power of words. They also believed that another form of power was beauty. This was something neither the elder nor younger Kincheloe had to worry about. Now I'm not saying they were hideous, but they certainly weren't no Brad Pitt or the boy that plays Thor. Thankfully, Klayton got his good looks from his mama and his great uncle. Wisely, they relied on their gift of communication. Some call it the gift of gab. They strongly believed that their God-given gift should be used, even if that use was for personal gain.

"May God have mercy on your poor, foolish soul for not using the gifts He gave you to get rich!" "You're gonna have to account to the Almighty Himself for why you squandered such a blessing."

These were a couple of Klayton's daddy and granddaddy's philosophies. Both his father and grandfather made it explicitly clear that they'd rather use their gift and be judged by God for using it for personal gain than to die poor and destitute and not have used it at all.

They really believed they would be able to endure God's judgment for some of their most unethical and immoral lapses in judgement.

They were very obtuse men in their way of thinking. They had amassed a fortune and built an empire in real estate and trading commerce both internationally and within the United States. They also owned railroad companies and tobacco fields. They invested in textile goods and owned a slew of hotels, grocery chains and various other businesses. If it made money, it made perfect sense for them to be involved in it. The Kincheloes, Pervis and Avril had gained a reputation for being very shrewd businessmen in all of their affairs. While they were very dominant and astute in their business transactions, they were actually quite personable in their day-to-day dealings amongst most of the common folk. They weren't overt racists, but they didn't care for the mixing of the races. It didn't so much bother them, as long as none of their children dated outside of their race.

They believed Blacks were ok if they stayed in their place, meaning that no nigger would ever be president of any of their companies, and certainly no nigger would ever get a promotion in their company solely on the basis they were Black and or educated. (Their sentiments, not mine.) There were ways around all these equal rights legislation and discrimination accusations with a simple phone call. Besides, they knew a lot of powerful people in prominent positions who owed them a few favors. They weren't about to play politics with these folks. When it came down to it, the Kincheloes were swift to remind these prominent men that they were merely public servants and who they really worked for. What's understood don't need to be discussed.

They say there's somebody for everybody. Enter, Ms. Abigail Lou 'Ella Wyndreft. She was every man's desire in just about all of Danville and three counties over in every direction. Ms. Abigail was what you'd call a Southern Peach. Part of the Southern Social elite. She was practically groomed for the likes of Klayton. From the time they started dating, there weren't many of Klayton's friends (albeit there weren't many) who didn't swoon over Ms. Abigail. And why not? She was tall, blonde, and athletic. Had piercing greenish-blue eyes, and a laugh that sounded like every man's favorite song. Her father had been a business partner of Avril's for many years.

Being a part of high society, it only seemed fitting for the children of families of their stature to mingle with one another. Klayton's mother and Abigail's mother belonged to the same bridge club that met every Thursday evening without fail. Well, after so many meetings and establishing a comfortable rapport with one another they thought it'd be just darling to have the kids accompany each other to the highly prestigious St. Cecilia Society Debutante ball in Charleston, SC. Both families owned homes in Charleston and thought offenses certainly would be taken by not allowing their young'uns to make an appearance. While neither of them cared to go, it was a way to get away from their parents fussing over them about everything they thought was fuss-worthy; which was anything, which was really nothing, but was everything to them. The product of only producing one child.

They had known each other for a few years prior to the ball but had never paid one another much attention. They were far too young at the time. They'd seen each other at different social gatherings such as carnivals and picnics that weren't open to the public. The events were private, invite-only affairs that their fathers paid for.

After the ball, Klayton and Abigail took a genuine liking to one another and formally started dating. This was shortly before Klayton's parents had split up. Abigail was very supportive in her role as a girlfriend. Though she couldn't fathom the gamut of emotions Klayton was experiencing, she tried to be there for him best as she knew how. Her family dynamics were quite different. Her parents adamantly disagreed with the idea of divorce. Though, they could envision the benefits of having their daughter tied to the glorified Kincheloe family. Had it not been for their parents making their acquaintance before the break-up, Klayton and Abigail's relationship would've been forbidden altogether.

Yeah, Abigail and Ol' King got along just fine. They were engaged to be married in the spring of 2020 but the pandemic of everyone's nightmares hit the world over and put a damper on their plans for an elaborate and grandiose wedding. It was postponed indefinitely, or at least until the mask mandate was lifted. As if Abigail wasn't envied enough by her peers already; the 6.82-carat diamond ring sure didn't help matters.

Ms. Abigail and Klayton would frequently go on romantic picnics together. Abigail did most of the planning, but it was Klayton who had the means to get them wherever they wanted to go. Sometimes Klayton would have the pilot fire up the helicopter and buzz around the skies of various counties for several hours, eating whatever Abigail put in the basket for them. There were times when they'd aimlessly coast up and down the Roanoke River, listening to Spotify and singing along to their favorite Ed Sheeran, Taylor Swift and Billie Eilish songs. They enjoyed each other's company. They'd exchange stories of things they'd done while they were away at college with friends. Abigail always seemed to be a bit more intrigued by the foolishness of Klayton's antics. Probably because he always got away with things he did, while she on the other hand, always seemed to find herself in the Dean's office explaining how she wound up in these various predicaments. Neither one of them feared consequences because of their family's affiliations with the schools they went to. Their fathers sat on the school boards and made hefty contributions and donations to the universities they attended.

Abigail earned a Bachelor's degree from Rice University, which is referred to as the Harvard of the South. Well, one of them anyway. Klayton attended The Citadel, his father's and grandfather's alma mater. Abigail returned home before continuing her education and receiving her Master's degree at Duke University in North Carolina. Her parents insisted she change schools. They thought it would be best for her to be closer to home and finish up her schooling there. They knew the trouble she was getting into at Rice and well, quite frankly, her father's reputation was at stake, and he'd protect it at all costs as well as to spare himself any embarrassment.

It was settled, so, she returned home immediately after earning her Bachelor's degree at Rice. Her father also sweetened the pot by gifting her a brand-new convertible Mercedes Benz with a Shih Tzu Pomeranian puppy in the passenger seat. She immediately fell in love with Mr. Snootles, as she had named him. The Mercedes wasn't bad either! Mr. Snootles wasn't the biggest fan of Klayton but the feeling was mutual. They tolerated one another, but they both loved Abigail and pretty much came to a truce when it came to sharing her. There were times, however, when they found themselves competing for her attention in the most unconventional ways.

On one evening in particular, Abigail was preparing to go out for a celebratory dinner with Klayton and couldn't seem to locate her beautiful, four-carat diamond and blue sapphire tennis bracelet (a gift from Klayton), who happened to arrive as she was searching for it. She answered the door in her satin robe and as she fitted one earring in place, she reluctantly explained the situation,

"King, honey, now I don't want you to panic because I know it's here somewhere and besides, I just saw my bracelet earlier today, but I can't remember if I set it on the vanity in my closet or left it sitting on the end table near the sofa in the bonus room. Do you mind taking a peek in there for me honey, please, while I finish getting dressed so we're only fashionably late for our reservation? Which you did make, right honey?"

"Sure, I'll take a look and of course I did!" Klayton squawked, rubbing his palm across the back of his neck in an attempt to keep cool. He grimaced in response to the news of the missing bracelet.

The truth of the matter was he'd forgotten to make the reservation, which wasn't good for him because this was one of the hottest restaurants in town. On average there was a two-month wait for reservations; didn't matter what night of the week it was. If you didn't know somebody such as the owner, head chef or Maître de, you didn't stand a chance of getting in without a reservation. As it happened, Klayton knew all of 'em. So, as he went to search for the bracelet, he placed a call to the owner, Girard Castillon (might as well start at the top) and requested the best table in the house. "That would be no problem, sir!" Girard replied, and just like that, it was done.

Girard owed much of his success to Klayton...the food was exquisite at Le Grand Cadieux (The Big Little Castle) but between pushing permits through in the early days and landing him his prime location, Girard knew who to thank, and how to show his gratitude when his restaurant shot to the top.

After calling in his favor, Klayton actually became invested in looking for this missing bracelet. After all, he did pay for it. As he turned the corner and entered the bonus room, he saw the expensive piece of jewelry glistening while dangling from the mouth of Mr. Snootles. As he approached the dog, Mr. Snootles backed away and growled. Klayton tried a gentler approach.

"C'mon boy! Bring it to Papa! C'mon now!" Mr. Snootles continued to growl and back away, taunting him as though it was a game. But this was no game as far as Klayton was concerned and, quite frankly, he was starting to lose his patience. He gave chase to the small pooch that took off with lightning speed out of the bonus room and down the hall heading straight for the powder room near the front entrance.

"Not the powder room, not the powder room!"

He could hear Abigail yell in the distance, "Did you see it at all sugar plumb? I wish you'd do what I asked you to do before you come in and start playing with the dog!"

"I'm working on it, honey!"

The dog scurried into the powder room with his tail end jack-knifing behind him, attempting to regain control after sliding on the hard-wood floors. Klayton stood in the doorway, panting and bracing himself with his hands on both sides of the doorframe as he chose his words carefully in between breaths,

"Alright na, listen Mr. Snootles," Klayton was panting much like a dog himself,

"I'm gonna make you a proposition." He paused to catch his breath. "You give me the very expensive toy you have so I can give it to Mama, and I'll give you a treat, ok? How 'bout that?" He waved at the dog to come to him. The small ball of fur continued his low growl and positioned himself closer to the toilet. Klayton could see that psychology wasn't working in his favor. His fear became more prevalent as the dog perched himself up on his hind legs against the toilet. King's $115,000.00 purchase was dangerously dangling above the abyss.

If Klayton didn't act quickly, his extravagant gift was close to becoming a memory. He inched closer to the dog and thought to himself, *"it's now or never."* His heart was pounding nearly out of his chest. He lunged with his arm extended and his hand open. The dog yelped, but Klayton plunged his hand into the toilet, anticipating the bracelet falling from the dog's mouth into his hand. Mr. Snootles jumped nearly four feet into the air and landed with cat-like reflexes, dashing out of the powder room and straight into Abigail's arms.

She exclaimed, "Hey there, baby! Hey there! What 'cha got there? Oh, my Lord! You got Mama's bracelet? You found Mama's bracelet? You're such a good boy! Honey! Mr. Snootles found my bracelet!"

Just then, Klayton turned the corner with half his sleeve dripping toilet water.

"Yeah, so I heard."

"Now how is it that you couldn't find it but he could?" She continued to praise Mr. Snootles, rubbing his belly and allowing him to lick her wildly on her cheeks. "What were you doing anyway? And why is your sleeve all wet? Oh, never mind! Klayton, honey, you're dripping water all over my alpaca rug! You play entirely too much! We gotta get going sugar plumb, you know how busy they get at the little castle!"

CHAPTER 2
Put Up or Shut Up!

Now Klayton came up in a different era than his father and grandfather. He was from the current regime of racists that have no shame in letting it be known that it's quite alright to hate your neighbor. Especially those who don't look like you, or those who hold a different opinion from yours. He admired those that were in some of the highest positions of political power and fanned the flames of racial inequality and injustice. He even supported a certain political figure who quickly became famous for spewing mindless hatred on a daily basis, either out of his mouth or on social media. This king of the hill, at the time, spent more time on social media than he actually did fulfilling the duties of the office he was elected to. He was a staunch proponent in the promotion of bigotry, hatred, oppression, white supremacy, and discrimination. Violence on top of violence.

Inciting riots and placing bounties on the American military (allegedly); A whole mess of confusement and communism...communism? Now hold on one damn minute! Not communism! Even Klayton had a limit, and being a communist was beyond it. He believed in Mom, the military, the 2nd Amendment, baseball (and even that was becoming too Black for him) and of course apple pie. But back door, back room, backstabbing deals against America and the military that defends everything precious to it, was crossing the line. He didn't give a damn who you were!

Klayton had been feeling like the world was being handed over to Blacks, Hispanics, and Asians. While the Jews were just downright greedy som'bitches. (His sentiments not mine.) He started taking notice shortly after he finished college at The Citadel and went back home to Danville, VA. He saw the world was changing and he didn't like it. He saw the laws changing and they were working against the White man to give Blacks and Mexicans handouts or, as they liked to say, "Level the playing field". No one wanted to work hard for anything anymore like his father and grandfather and great-grandfather did to build this great nation. Notice I didn't mention him.

As far as he was concerned these people were becoming too sophisticated and educated to actually work for what they wanted. Instead, they relied on the skills they acquired to swindle the system out of positions and money. The government was going soft and being pushed in a direction quite different from his ancestors' days of influence. So, it was up to him to do something about it. He had to change things if he wanted to restore power, dignity and respect to the White race, the supreme race. That's when the PMG was conceptualized. Now you might wonder, where does a man of Klayton's stature find the time to concern himself with such things? Well, I've pondered the same thing a time or two myself… and the answer is quite simple. When you have money like the Kincheloes, there's hardly anything you actually *have* to do. You do what all lazy folk do… you get someone else to do it for you. Isn't that how slavery started in the first place? Man, history sure does have a funny way of repeating itself, doesn't it? The more things change, the more they stay the same.

Anyhow, the world was moving into an age where technological advancements were growing in leaps and bounds which included scientific advancements. Tracing your biological roots as far back as the early 16th century or further was common place nowadays. Klayton was well aware of services existing to find out about your ancestral roots. He was ready to swab, spit, sweat, bleed, pee or do whatever he had to do to prove he was of the purest race on the face of the earth. He held himself at the highest level of accountability and would accept nothing less of his brethren of the PMG.

He ordered 200 DNA kits from "EZ DNA-123" with his own money. Actually, he had somebody else order them, but he did foot the bill. Even though the PMG only had 25 members, he was certain that number was about to drastically increase. The price of the kits was not an obstacle. In fact, he was proud he could do this for his brothers as a late Christmas gift. Although, that's all he had ever given them. He just enjoyed the accolades of doing something that meant so much to himself.

In all actuality, the rest of the kits were on reserve for future members, or in case one of the current members messed theirs up. But if they needed a replacement, it'd be at their own expense. First of anything is always free. This was part of the Kincheloe creed. The shipment of DNA kits were delivered to the Kincheloe estate in Westover Hills where Klayton eagerly awaited their arrival from the courier. He slipped a crisp twenty-dollar bill in the driver's work shirt pocket for loading the boxes onto the bed of his pick-up truck.

He was a parsimonious son-of-a-gun but boy was he excited! He even called over two of his buddies and co-chairs of the PMG, Davis and Dallas Bostitch, to help him stock the supply room with their newly acquired requisite devices. Their PMG meetings were held in a stock room of one of Klayton's supermarkets. It wasn't actively being used as a stockroom because it was one of the stores that was burnt down during civil unrest in Danville in the mid-sixties. The stockroom was the only thing that survived the fire due to the materials that were used to construct it. It was built initially to act as a reinforced shelter for tornadoes. His father, Avril Kincheloe, decided to keep the stockroom because he was impressed with its durability and rebuilt the main store.

Many believed that the elder Kincheloe, my brother Pervis, paid to have the store torched for an insurance payout, but that was never proven. It was whispered among friends, but no one ever dared mutter it loud enough to be heard by Pervis himself. If they were thinking it, they'd better be careful not to be moving their lips too much. The stockroom was where a lot of the Kincheloe business deals were conspired and only God knows what else. But after the two older gentlemen handed the reins over to the younger Kincheloe, not many business transactions took place there. It served as more of a hangout or a clubhouse for Klayton and his buddies to come up with whatever hair-brained schemes their hearts desired.

Well, like this one time they thought it'd be a good idea to round up the local colored citizens' animals and hold 'em hostage in the stockroom. King and his cronies theorized, which was completely unfounded and couldn't be further from the truth if I may add, that these animals were wild and untrained, much like their owners. I reckon these numbskulls hadn't taken into account that the animals they'd stolen wasn't gonna go silently, but also, they weren't gonna stay quiet either. They could only hold onto'em for a few hours before they had to let them go. But that's beside the point! If I can insert an idiom here to paint you a picture of those idiots, those cats and dogs fought like, well…cats and dogs, clawing and biting them boys up something fierce! When the police interviewed them, they lied and said they didn't know a thing about it. It didn't help their case with Clete and Dallas not being able to stop scratching during questioning. Like many of the pets' owners, I wasn't too thrilled either about them boys giving those poor cats and dogs fleas either.

    It was finally time to show his brothers what he was made of, and them to him as well. Klayton could hardly contain himself. He thought taking this test would solidify his place in history amongst the great White men that came before him and the ones to come after the ones he would help mold. This would not only prove that White was the purest race but the superior one as well. So long as it wasn't mixed or contaminated by *the others.*

Klayton called a meeting for 6:45 in the p.m. to distribute the kits to all members and aspiring ones too. Well, after all, it was required that you take the test before being considered or remaining a member. Klayton issued the Bostitch boys twenty-five kits to hand out to all attendees. It was mid-January and what better way to start the year off right than to prove you were White?

Klayton entered the stockroom first, followed by Dallas, Davis and then Cletus Farmbrooke, who was pretty much Klayton's right-hand man when it came to dealing with sensitive matters of the PMG. Klayton wasn't very trusting, and he felt the Bostitch boys were idiots but were good to have around for a few laughs. Besides they made good henchmen. But things of a serious nature concerning real business and attention had to be left in the hands of someone competent like himself. Besides, Clete had a degree in law and graduated in the top 3% of his class from Harvard, but he never passed the bar so he couldn't practice.

Either way, he was quite well-versed and stayed abreast of current local statutes and ordinances. Of course, he was an asset to Klayton who made his life comfortable, and he kept Klayton aware of the legal ramifications he might endure if he and the boys got a little too rowdy. Which they were known to do from time to time. Now rumor had it, Ol' King and some of the boys would leave the stockroom after slamming a few pints apiece and terrorize a few of the colored neighborhood locals. They'd urinate in the empty bottles and smash them against their cars and houses and even pursue them in their vehicles while dangling nooses out the windows of their trucks, yelling obscenities and waving confederate flags.

Well, it was approaching seven o'clock and the rest of the boys were strolling in slowly but surely. As the men came in, they were greeted by Davis at the door who pointed them to a table that was set up in the corner and manned by Dallas who took attendance and issued everyone a kit and had them sign for it. As everyone took their seats and got settled in, the gavel loudly struck the wooden base 3 times in quick succession and the meeting was officially called to order by none other than Klayton Kincheloe himself.

"Alright, alright. Order, order! You boys simmer on down now, hear? This meeting is officially called to order. We'll start off by discussing the business at hand and then we'll open the floor up for questions and concerns as well as address some old business. As you know, the purpose of our meeting tonight is to administer these DNA kits and ship'em off. We'll wait for the results to come back and begin to increase our membership. Or decrease it, if need be, if your results come back unfavorably." Snickering could be heard around the room. "Now I don't imagine that should be a problem for none of ya's. But if it is, well…we'll just have to deal with that the way we deal with things." More snickering and now snorting could be heard.

A few more giggles and some snorting could be heard throughout the crowd. One member raised his hand and was acknowledged by Klayton, "Whaddya- got, Jesse?"

"Well, King, me and a few of the boys was having a discussion and was wondering just how necessary something like this really is? I mean, I ain't questioning your authority or even your leadership. Hell, you know we behind you 100% whatever it is you decide, but this D and A kit ain't gon' change nothing. We who we gon' be and always have been."

"Now look-a here, I know a few of you boys got some apprehensions 'bout this test and all. For the record Jesse, it's a D-N-A kit not a D and A kit, but nonetheless, it's absolutely vital for all of y'all to take this test to prove to your brothers here that you belong and that you are a pure American. Our heritage is at stake here and that is especially important! I refuse to stand by idly while the PMG gets infiltrated by impure contaminants. We will not be one of those organizations that allow any and everybody in. Dammit, we do discriminate! It is our God-given right to filter and sift out those that are trying to make us the minority! Hardly anything in America is sacred anymore. It has to start somewhere…Dammit, I say why not here?" As his fist slams against the podium. Sporadic applause and *"Amen, brother!"* could be heard throughout the crowd.

"Now, I know you all are anxious and some of you got to get on back home to ya families, so let's just get this underway and the sooner we do, the sooner we all can be on our way. As far as you and a few of the boys getting together and brainstorming without me…well Jesse, that can be dangerous. That's why we meet here and discuss things openly.

These are the only closed doors needed. Y'all leave the figuring to me. That's if you really trust me like you say you do and all. I ain't never steered you boys wrong before, have I?"

Jesse replied, "Naw King, you ain't."

"Alright then, now we gon' do this in an orderly fashion so we can keep moving right along. Now that y'all got your kits. The process is fairly simple. Open up the box, take out the tube, spit in the tube with the pink liquid in the bottom of it, close the cap, give it a nice shake and put it back in the pouch. Seal it up and hand it off to one of these fine gents standing up here with me and we'll be off to the races. Now, if y'all would be so kind as to line up in single-file and start spitting in them tubes, I'd rightly appreciate it."

The process was moving right along until Amos Clearwater could be heard coughing and hacking so loud that everyone was certain he was at death's door. Nowadays, you can't cough without getting deadly looks and clearing a room, even if you're choking! But concerning Amos, he had been an avid smoker for the past 30 years or so. By his own account, he started when he was just seven years old. He'd sneak out the rear door of the school, usually to go fishing, and the janitor would be out back dumping trash or what-have-you.

One day they had an encounter and the janitor told him that he shouldn't be leaving school grounds on account he was so little and all, and if he continued, he'd have to report him. Well, Amos being Amos, he bargained with him and told him if he kept his mouth shut and gave him one of his smoke sticks, he'd keep quiet about seeing him pack extra bags of food while off-loading the delivery truck every week, that never seemed to make it to the pantry. Why, it was no wonder why *his portions* always seemed to be smaller than the other kids and why he was always left so hungry. On account of him being so little and all. There never seemed to be enough to go around when it came to him. The janitor caught his drift. The two agreed and from that day forward they became smoking buddies and exchanged stories but never once again mentioned the other one's indiscretions.

From that story alone, be it there were more, Amos became something of a local legend and gained a reputation for having as much dirt on you, if not more, than you had on him. Now if you got on his bad side, he had no problem with mule kicking over the whole damn pail of beans. Well, Amos' turn to hand in his kit came and he attempted to hand it off to Clete, but Clete shooed him with his hand and pointed to Davis, and Davis pointed to Dallas. Dallas had briefly turned to assist another fella and upon turning back around, was greeted by Amos holding a bag that looked as disgusting as it sounded when he was filling the tube. Dallas declared, "How in God's holy name he get a baby in there? That's gotta be a toddler or the world's biggest loogie! This som'bitch just gave birth through his pie hole! Don't make me no never-mind, cause I ain't touching it!" The room erupted with laughter.

It was finally the mastermind's turn, but not without a subtle urging from Clete, "Alright, alright na boys, y'all simmer on down now. Simmer on down now, hear?"

"Last but certainly not least," remarked Klayton. Klayton spits in the vial and gave it a strong shake, sealed it shut and the deal was done.

The meeting adjourned shortly afterward and there were smiles, handshakes and pats on the back all around. Klayton and the Bostitch boys placed the kits onto Klayton's pick-up bed and he drove off into the night. The next day Klayton was up early, bright-eyed and bushy-tailed raring to go to the post office. After he had mailed his precious cargo, he rightly didn't know what to do with himself until the results came back. He was told it would take anywhere between 3-12 weeks.

He tried to contain himself the best he could by visiting some of his businesses, but that grew old after the first few days. He was overwhelmed with frustration concerning the logistics of how the businesses operated. He had hired a bright, burgeoning young man to handle such matters. They were tedious tasks that he'd rather not be bothered with because the truth of the matter was, he was only concerned with the bottom line…the money. Not just the money, but the profits. He didn't like losing money under any circumstances.

King wasn't concerned about the employees, what hardships they might endure or their morale. Many of his employees were generational inheritors of their positions. There was plenty of nepotism to go around, as well as favoritism and flat-out discrimination. Klayton ran his businesses pretty much like he ran the PMG. The vast majority of Klayton's employees were Caucasian, by design, but due to the sheer size of his empire, there were quite a few minorities working for him as well. The tapestry of his companies had been woven together from the fibers of a systemically racist society that he loved, supported and proudly wore like a hand stitched quilt. Just as his father, grandfather and great-grandfather did before him.

    He spent the next several Sundays attending church services and wondering if he had amassed enough of a fortune to afford the most luxurious part of Heaven. In his mind he knew everybody loved money, even God. Why, He invented it, didn't He? Also, in his mind he figured that God was more partial to him because he was doing something meaningful with his life. He was using his gift. He thought, surely God wouldn't put him in the position he was in if he wasn't going to be accepted into Heaven with open arms. He was from the best race of them all.

CHAPTER 3
Misfortune

While Klayton didn't spend an enormous amount of time in church as an adult, he had spent quite a bit of time in one as a child. He, like many children growing up with a spiritual upbringing, was made to attend Sunday services every week: Beginning with the morning service, only to return for the evening service. That was a given. So, like many older teenagers, when he was old enough to make his own decision on the matter, he decided not to go. Well, not as much anyway. He still would go with his mother on occasion. He and his mother were very close, though their relationship became strained when she left his father. He understood that decision to some degree. He loved his mother dearly and respected and trusted her reasons for leaving if she felt that's what she needed to do. He knew firsthand that his father was not an easy man to love because he loved money more than he loved people. A wife and a son could feel those priorities inherently. Klayton and his mother were a lot alike in that regard.

Klayton's father was 16 years older than his mother. Many people thought that she was too young to be married when they became engaged, but she was smitten, just as many of the young women who worked for my nephew Avril. But Miriam Blanchette Kincheloe was different from those other women in the sense that she wasn't impressed with his money or power. She admired how much confidence he spoke with regarding business issues. But his social awkwardness couldn't be hidden from her, no matter how hard he tried to conceal it. She was quite intrigued as to why he was interested in her. She was a simple girl: not needy, or forward, but always carried herself like a lady. Dignified and graceful with class and elegance. The other women came across as loose and obsequious in her opinion. Miriam was always cool, calm and collected.

That was really what attracted Avril to her. Initially, she wouldn't give him the time of day. The more she refused, the more he pursued her until one day he came right out and said as he leaned on her desk smiling,

"This is the very last time that I'm gonna ask you to go out with me or show the slightest amount of interest in you. After that, I'll never ask you again and we'll both have to wonder

'What if-?' for the rest of our lives."

"Great! Sounds like a plan to me. Because I was just thinking, *while it's obvious he's a very smart businessman, it's just as obvious he's not a very bright man.*" No one had ever dared to speak to him in such a manner. He was equally appalled and intrigued at the same time.

There was a brief moment of silent staring between them before they both burst out in laughter. From that moment forward they were inseparable, or at least until Klayton's 17th birthday, which was around the time she left.

From the holy law, he had been taught he'd have to forgive his mom for hurting him by leaving.

However, he also had to forgive his father for hurting her. It was the right thing to do, especially if he wanted to be forgiven himself, so he did it. As much as it hurt for his family to be torn apart, he knew that his parents' relationship had developed into a contentious one. They argued more than they talked and hardly ever agreed on anything. It had become quite clear that Avril's primary concern had become his businesses and that's what seemed to bring him true happiness. His parents' split was amicable and decent; he had that to be grateful for at least. It didn't drag out in court with proceedings and drama.

In his own way, Avril still loved and cared for Miriam deeply. In the divorce proceedings, Avril gave her two homes free and clear. One in Portsmouth, VA and one in Wellesley, MA. On top of that, there was $15,000,000.00 in cash, half a dozen properties along the Eastern Coast for residual income and child support. And it was still just a drop in the bucket for him. Klayton remained with him, even though it was only less than a year. It was how he worked it out with the courts and Miriam. He knew people. If it were up to her, she would've left just as she had come. She would've walked away with nothing but the clothes on her back and the shoes on her feet. She didn't ask him for anything, but he offered, so she accepted. She wasn't a fool either.

Klayton's drive and determination to get what he wanted, no matter the cost was without a doubt inherited from his father. Whatever he wanted, he got and he'd let nothing deter him from it. On the other hand, his wit and charm came from his mother. He knew how to use all of his attributes to get just about anything he wanted in life.

The moment of truth had finally arrived. It felt like an eternity waiting for the results of the DNA kits to arrive, but in reality, it had only taken 6 weeks. King cared about no one's results more than his own. He was going to set the bar high. He pitied those who would inevitably receive unfavorable results. Those contaminated with Black, Hispanic, Asian, Native American and all the other kinds of blood that weren't of the pure breed. Why, he could just imagine himself sitting on the throne of power while banishing the paupers from his presence, "No! Get out of here! Banish yourself from my presence! Never return to the prestigious

PMG!" He couldn't contain the smirk as his internal dialect got the best of him.

The word went out that the meeting would be held at 1 pm. However, the venue had been changed. Ol' King wanted this to be a memorable and special event, so he planned for it to be at the family estate, his very own home. This was far too important for the likes of the stockroom. Hell, he even sprung for himself a new suit with shoes to match. He had Ms. Abigail picked up and brought to the house in his brand-new Bentley. He spared no expense for the occasion. He had staff on standby to answer his guests' every beck and call, even though he was only serving hors d'oeuvres. It wasn't like he was rolling out the red carpet for these boys. As far as he was concerned, they should all just be grateful he allowed them on the premises, fed them fancy finger foods, and paid his workers for serving them.

Ordinarily King would go first as always with everything, and with this especially, seeing how revved up he was. But he had become distracted by a minor disturbance in the butler's pantry amongst a few of the servants. There was a bit of confusion as to what wine was to be served. However, they were all wrong because King had no intention of serving any wine at all. He instructed them to serve his guests some grape muscadine juice, which he reminded them was a constituent of wine, but he'd be damned and stretched a hundred different ways from Sunday if he was going to serve these freeloading bastards any of his top-shelf libations. They'd be lucky to get the bad batches of shine he and the Bostich boys cooked up here and there.

Liddy, his senior housemaid, informed him in her most polite voice, "Mr. Kincheloe, sir, this grape juice is expired and Josiah ain't been around to collect the whole lot to get rid of 'em yet. What'cha want me to serve 'em instead?"

"Serve 'em instead? Instead of what, water? And why the hell ain't Josiah been 'round here to pick 'em up yet? You mean to tell me he got paid for services not rendered?"

Liddy clasped her hands together and shifted her eyes towards the floor, "I don't know sir, I think he got sick or something. Maybe he got hold of some bad grape juice." As other staff members chuckled, Klayton curtly replied, "Liddy, I hear you sass-mouthing me but because I got other pressing matters to tend to, I'm gon' give ya a pass this one time. Give it to 'em anyway."

"Now Mr. Kincheloe sir we can't have these people getting sick on account you knowingly gave 'em expired grape juice! That ain't right!"

"Consider it fermented. What's understood don't need to be discussed. Liddy, serve our guests. G'wone na… G'wone!" Liddy sighed heavily and spun around on her heels in an about face gesture and reluctantly responded,

"Yes sir, Mr. Kincheloe."

Before his brief departure to deal with all the confusion, he had instructed Clete to go ahead and conduct the business at hand. Clete, being similar in nature to Klayton, started with his results first. Klayton had set up a projector so each member could place his phone underneath and as the app opened, the ancestry results would be shared on a huge screen for all to witness. He had sternly warned all members against reviewing their results before the meeting. He spoke of honor, and intestinal fortitude, and theirs would be called into question if they peeked before sharing this moment with their brethren. They all had looked at their results before they arrived, but they played along as if they hadn't.

Well, all of them except Clete. He looked up to Klayton and held him in high regard, so he honored Klayton's wishes. Clete proudly read his results aloud for all to hear. Of course, he hadn't blurted out anything before scanning it quickly with his eyes first. He exclaimed, "Now, you can't get more white, I mean right, than this! Hell, it's all the same anyway, ain't it? White equals right!" There was laughter in unison as he held up his fist, pumping it high in the air proudly, as he collected his phone and moved on. His results read: 84% European, 12% Australian, 2% New Zealand, 0.3% Scandinavian and so forth and so forth to round out the totality of his makeup. He didn't concern himself with anything other than the vast majority of the results showing that he was predominantly Caucasian. Everything else was trivial to him and he could remain a member in good standing.

Dallas went next followed by his brother Davis, then Gromer Hanslow, another local townsman, and then Jesse and several others. By this time, they were just about halfway through the reading of all the results. A couple of the boys were feeling the heat as their results were inconclusive and would have to be taken again. If they were allowed to. Ol' King would decide if they were worthy or not.

It was finally King's time to shine. His good buddy Clete gave a brief introduction for their gracious host. "Now, we been patiently waiting for our fearless leader to grace us with his results, which I'm sure is nothing but a formality at this point. But rules are rules, and without further ado, I give you our brother, our leader and visionary, Mr. Klayton "King" Kincheloe!"

Applause filled the air as Klayton took to the center of the room with his phone in hand. He confidently approached the projector. He glanced up and smiled at Ms. Abigail who returned the pleasantry, standing front and center, arm in arm with Clete. While it was a gentlemanly gesture by anyone's account, after all this was the South, where chivalry was not dead, it was Clete's innermost desire for this to be more than what it was at first glance. Clete coveted nothing more than to be head of the PMG and to have Ms. Abigail by his side as his own companion.

Klayton confidently slid his phone under the projector and opened the DNA app. After the app finished loading, his eyes appeared to dilate and bulge simultaneously. He immediately became drenched with sweat. His mouth went dry as cotton. He could not believe what his eyes were seeing. Gasps erupted across the room as if the air had been sucked right out of it. Dishes crashed and shattered after hitting the marble floor. After a brief moment of reverie, curses began to be heard, muttered under the breath of incredulous once-brothers, betrayed by the one who called himself their leader.

"Alright now, this ain't funny!" Shouted one of the inconclusives, in a feeble attempt to display solidarity. Ms. Abigail briefly fainted and Clete was obliged to hold her up and fan her with a sweaty hand. All the while, Klayton fought with every ounce of strength in his body to keep his legs from buckling underneath him. He held on tightly to the cart that held the projector while bracing himself. He attempted to gain focus through the tears as he stared at the tiny screen of his phone while his fiancée and brothers ogled the giant screen emblazoned with: 73% European, 4% Reykjavik,

11% Cameroon, 5% Gabonese, 4% Kenyan, 0.5% Sioux Indian, 0.4% Norwegian and the rest didn't even matter. It stopped mattering once his eyes dismissively grazed across the other ethnicities and honed in on the measly 73% European. He was 100% crushed! Absolutely devastated! What did this mean for Ol' King? I tell ya what it meant.

It meant he was only a portion of what he thought he was. But by everyone else's account, he was full of it! Whatever *it* was. It also meant somebody had some explaining to do!

There were no words to describe the betrayal that Klayton's brothers felt. They were outraged! Klayton struggled to collect himself and attempted to explain that there must have been a grave error made on behalf of the company he used to test the kits. There just had to be something wrong. Klayton even tried to convince the boys that his kit had been mixed up with someone else's, perhaps one of those inconclusives amongst them in the crowd. Tampered with even. Those boys weren't buying any of it. Ol' King was grasping for straws, and every one of 'em had gotten shorter with every reach. He made claims that someone *had* to have hacked into his account with EZ-DNA-123. He was going to sue them into oblivion…if he didn't own the company already or a significant number of shares in it. Someone had to be held accountable for this travesty! He was convinced that he was the target of a cruel, elaborate prank. To which he, like many of his PMG buddies, failed to see the humor.

If there had been anybody there that wanted to console him, he would've been inconsolable, but that person just didn't exist in this crowd. His denial was off the charts. There was just no way God would allow something this horrible to happen to him, of all people. How could God love him and let this happen to him? There had to be some logical explanation. He was determined to get to the bottom of this abomination if it was the last thing on earth he did!

His escape from his own home was a narrow one. With the help of Liddy and a couple of other servants, he was somewhat reluctantly shuffled through the rear entrance of the kitchen by them, down a service corridor and out a side door. Liddy handed him the keys to her vehicle which was parked closer than his. After giving him the keys, she told him, "I know it ain't much, but bring her back in one piece. She's all I got for now." His rescuers seemed to agree that no one deserved to be attacked because of their ethnicity; a sentiment that, until that very moment, King would have shot down quicker than anyone.

Klayton had never been on this side of a fight. The man out-manned. The prey of a gang of hungry hot heads. The angry mob was in hot pursuit after their meeting had erupted. Glasses and food had been tossed with pure hatred, while curses were vehemently hurdled. He had the difficult task of processing how they turned on him so quickly. Just a few minutes before he had been a visionary and their fearless leader. Now he was public enemy number one, and they were trying to rip him to pieces.

He just didn't understand why he was being treated in this fashion; after all it's not like he had any control over what his make-up was. If there was any truth to it. It wasn't his fault...right? And furthermore, he still looked White...well sort of. Klayton glanced at his hand, gripping the steering wheel of the borrowed car. But he was the same on the inside...maybe. Perhaps his true colors were beginning to shine through. Maybe his skin appeared rosier than normal from all the excitement that just transpired. Yeah, that was it! He was flushed, that was what it had to be. He wasn't doing that great of a job convincing himself, but it was better than nothing. He knew exactly who he needed to speak with to make sense out of this nonsense. His parents. Of course, they'd be able to give him some kind of inkling as to what the hell was going on. They'd know exactly what to do!

Once he felt he was a safe distance from the violence that had nearly overtaken him, Klayton telephoned his mother and informed her he was on his way to her house. He needed to talk to her about the unfortunate circumstances that just unfolded, but it was very important he spoke with her face to face. She tried to get him to calm down and reassured him everything was going to be ok, but what did she know of the fierce hatred he'd just encountered? Then he called his father and relayed the same message, explaining he wanted to meet with him at his mother's house, but it had to be face to face to which his father agreed.

He needed answers, but he also just needed to go somewhere that he could think out loud. His options were limited. His home obviously wasn't available. Neither was Abigail's, or the stockroom.

It wouldn't be long before they showed up there looking for him. He had nowhere to go that he felt safe. In his own town for Christ's sakes! He decided to take all the back roads to get to his mother's house. He needed to give himself time to sort things out in his head, but her place was over three and a half hours away. He was sure he'd use all of that time to reflect on what was happening to him and why...he'd use every single second. But first, he called EZ-DNA-123 and let them have it. He minced no words when explaining what the consequences would be if they didn't fix this in the most expedient fashion. He demanded new kits be sent to him immediately at their expense and that the turn around on the results be expedited. He also contacted three other companies and ordered kits from them as well. He was leaving no stone unturned this go-around. He was livid!

His mind moved as fast as the car, along with the ill feeling in his gut which sank deeper. He couldn't for the life of him figure out how something like this could happen. For an instance, he danced with the idea that he did have black blood in him. The more he pondered that, the less it made sense. His thoughts ran unbridled in his head:

Black blood? No such thing exists, does it? All blood is red...isn't it? As a child I can remember hearing Rev. Cornwalis screaming, "Jesus' blood is the only blood that matters!" Could one of my parents have had an affair? What if my father really wasn't my biological father? Maybe that's why they really divorced! What if my mother was actually a Black woman who my father had an affair with and Miriam, being the only mother I've ever known, was nothing more than a stand-in for my real mother who was banished because of the scandalous nature of her and my father's relationship? Maybe I was adopted?

None of it made any sense to him but it didn't stop the thoughts from churning like fresh whipped butter. Glancing once again at his fists clutching the steering wheel, it occurred to him that his skin had always appeared slightly darker than both of his parents and he'd always tan so easily. He would get plenty of compliments on his tan upon returning from vacation with his family. He appeared darker than his cousins when they gathered for family events. Everyone could always tell when he'd been to Naples, Bordeaux or Florida. He dismissed all of those possibilities; they were ridiculous, absurd and stupid and there was just no way he was going to be Black.

CHAPTER 4
Kindred Encounters

After driving for some time, King was famished and needed to stop and get a bite to eat. He pulled into the town of Emporia, Virginia to a small diner, 'Snooze and Lou's with a subtitle that read, "Welcome! Southern hospitality starts here, c'mon in!"

While he was certainly no stranger to extreme heat, being from Danville and all, but what he was experiencing inside the small diner was a different kind of heat altogether. It felt familiar, but deep down on his insides King knew that it was just in his mind.

By now it was mid-April, and the days were already sizzling hot. The diner was filled but not over-crowded. Natural light poured into the huge floor-to-ceiling windows at the front entrance. The further you went to the rear, the less light there was. The long fluorescent ceiling lights did little to help, still casting shadows on the faces of the patrons. Ceiling fans, surprisingly quiet, twirled at the highest speeds in an attempt to combat the environmental temperature as well as the body heat of the occupants. Those in attendance were neighborhood regulars, and by their conversations it was obvious they were a tight-knit group. They were clearly familiar with each other and could tell when a stranger was amongst them. Klayton took a seat at the end of the bar. He noticed not all but several patrons were wearing masks. He didn't care because he wasn't wearing a mask under any circumstances, mandate or not. He looked at the single laminated front-and-back menu and was delightfully surprised to see there were chicken gizzards available.

He couldn't pass this up. Why, he hadn't had chicken gizzards since Bessie Mae made them for him and her boys when he was just a young'un himself. That woman could cook!

Talk about gifts, cooking was definitely hers. Bessie Mae served as head cook for many years for my brother Pervis, and whenever Klayton went to visit, which was frequently, Ol' Bessie Mae would whip him and her boys up a batch of gizzards and send them on out to play in the field. He couldn't get enough of them. They were quite tasty. Klayton sat there in the diner and briefly revisited his childhood by simply looking at the words on the menu, "In this part of the South, love is served from our hearts to your mouth!" The description enticed him even more that read, "Tender, crispy, golden, hand-battered, deep-fried chicken gizzards." Boy that was a mouthful, and he couldn't wait 'til his was stuffed full of gizzards. He started off unconsciously smiling, but once aware, he continued.

He thought about the word love and how it fit into his childhood. He questioned, "Did it fit?" He wondered if he had been missing out on it all this time. The uproar from his brethren of the PMG certainly didn't feel like love. Even their lightly-held devotion hadn't felt very loving when it existed. He quietly thought to himself, if he'd recognize love even if it grabbed hold of him and shook him real hard. He knew he felt something rather intense for Ms. Abigail, but was it really love? Besides his parents, he didn't know who loved him or who he loved outside of them. In his mind love seemed to be forever fleeting. He compared it to people, they come and go. His thoughts were, "Nothing lasts forever!" But little did Ol'King know, that couldn't be further from the truth.

While he wasn't sure of much right now, Klayton was certain of one thing, and that was he had to have those gizzards. What's understood don't need to be discussed! He eagerly placed his order and while he waited for his food, he surveyed the room. He could see several anxious faces, coupled with murmurs throughout the group. He wondered why, and did *he* bring the uneasiness in with him? No, it had to be something else...but what? Never accused of being shy, he posed the question to whoever in the room answered it, "Who died?"

A dark-skinned, wavy-haired man sitting a few feet away from him at a table with a couple of other patrons responded, "Nobody yet."

"Yet, what the hell you mean yet?"

"I mean 'yet' as in, you lookin' like you real close to death. You look like you ain't got no peace man, that's all I'm saying. Nothing more. It wasn't meant to be no threat. You just look tired and run-down. I can tell you ain't from 'round here, cause of how you dressed and that watch you wearing. Ain't nobody from 'round here rockin' no Rolex…you feel me? I see you into them Unicorns. I know my watches." Klayton's eyes darted down quickly at his watch and then back up without moving his head. The man paused briefly before continuing,

"What leads you to these parts anyway, if you don't mind me asking?"

"As a matter of fact, I do mind ya asking. It ain't none of ya damn business where I'm from." Klayton cautiously surveyed the room after that comment before continuing, once he saw no one had moved towards him. "You probably ain't never heard of it anyway. And if I wasn't so hungry, I wouldn't have even stopped in this God-forsaken hell hole! Speaking of hunger, where's my food at anyway?"

The curly-haired waitress replied, "It's coming up now, sir." Klayton replied sharply, "Bout damn time and don't forget my beer either."

"Of course not, sir." The curly-haired waitress wearing a nametag that read 'Sadie' picked up her pace behind the counter.

The dark-skinned, wavy-haired man joined in, "God ain't forsaken us, sir. He's a provider and He's faithful!" The room was filled with affirmations of *Amen! Yes, He is!* and the ever-popular, *Won't He do it?*

"I assume you all are talking about God, but do what?" Klayton interjected, "Cause whatever you think He's gonna do for you people, He obviously placed it low on His priority list. Don't look like He's been through this place in a nice long while, and if He ever was here, He ain't coming back! Well, any of y'all gon' answer my question 'bout who died? Everybody looking all sad and it ain't got nothing to do with me. Na, what gives?"

A voice shouted from the back, "Go ahead and tell him what's going on, Trey."

Trey was the dark-skinned, wavy-haired man. "Well sir, truth be told, we are doing a bit of grieving due to the *'appearance'* that we won't have enough money or volunteers to put on our annual Virginia pork festival this year. The festival usually runs every second week in June, and has for more than 40 years."

"Ah, so that explains the sign out front talking about donations being appreciated and all." Klayton wasn't impressed. "Pork festival? What you talking 'bout? Chitterlings?" Klayton attempted to be humorous and insulting simultaneously, but more of the latter.

"Na, what you know about chitterlings?" Trey countered.

"I know they stink up to the high heavens and I know I don't eat 'em!" Trey gave Klayton a dramatic roll of his eyes while pointing his phone in Klayton's direction, and matter-of-factly stated, "Na, what's understood don't need to be discussed. I know you ain't eating no chitterlings bruh."

Klatyon couldn't believe what he thought he heard, first his eyes now his ears.

"Wait a minute, what did you just say?"

"I said, I know you ain't eating no chit----."

Klayton abruptly cut him off before he could finish, "Naw, naw, naw, right before that. What's underst…"

"Oh that, I said, what's understood don't need to be discussed."

"Where'd you hear that from?" Klayton heard *his* words coming from another man's mouth.

"It's just something my daddy used to say all the time while he was workin' at the railroad company. Told me he used to hear this old guy say it whenever he came 'round."

"You talking 'bout CXS Norfolk Southern?"

"Yeah, used to be Norfolk and Western Railway." Trey eagerly welcomed the exchange.

"Yeah, yeah, yeah I know the family that owns it." As a side note, that would be OUR family he's talking 'bout.

"Na see, don't nobody that live 'round here own no railway company either, they just work there. That proves you ain't from around here."

Trey had hit a delicate nerve and Klayton responded with some of that heat he'd felt upon entering the diner. "Na look'a here, I don't take too kindly to wealth shaming. You people always looking for a handout or some type of government assistance program. Speaking of which, why don't ya just apply for a grant or something? Instead of playing on people's sympathy and begging!"

Trey responded, "Well sir, the turn-a-round time on processing a grant for a small-town festival would just take way too long and time ain't on our side. Have you ever filled out an application for a grant?" He waited with a patient smile, "I didn't think so...never mind. Besides, I don't recall nobody asking you for nothing except Sadie asking you what you wanna eat and me asking where you were from, and you took exception to that! As I mentioned earlier, God is a provider and He *is* faithful. He been providing for the last forty + years for this festival and I don't see no reason why He'd stop now. Delay isn't denial" The locals chimed in again, *"That's right! Preach Trey! Amen! Somebody better tell him!"* You could see a few of the towels they used to wipe their perspiring faces being waived as the affirmations were being shouted.

Trey continued, "In the words of the Pulitzer Prize winner, my man Ke--"

Klayton jumped in before Trey could finish with, "King! King, right? Dr. Martin Luther King...Jr...? Ain't that who you was gonna say?"

Trey responded with subtle laughter in his voice, while Sadie chuckled and shook her head along with several other patrons, "Naw man, the other Black guy; Kendrick Lamar, his song, 'We gon' be Alright'; two different men, two different awards. Dr. King won the Nobel Peace Prize, Kendrick Lamar won the Pulitzer Prize for music. I'm actually impressed though. I wouldn't have guessed you knew who Dr. King was, 'cause I know damn well you don't know who the other brother is!"

Klayton responded, "Oh yeah? Well, I had a dream too, that I ordered some food and it came up a hell of a lot quicker than this! You're a little stereotypical aren't ya?"

"Now you would know, wouldn't ya? You people...wealth shaming? Seriously? Wow!" The men looked at each other and shared a small chuckle, shaking their heads.

Ol' King couldn't understand why he felt so at ease here, but he did. Perhaps it was because he felt like he was just being a regular person. Even with him being the minority in this situation, he didn't feel threatened. He walked into this diner with the weight of the world on his shoulders and yet here he was, just talking to people and being sociable. As best as he knew how. And he enjoyed that feeling. He didn't feel any pressure to be anyone other than himself. Even though he was still trying to figure that part out. Not a CEO, not the leader of a group, not the perfect son. Just a person amongst other people. Nothing more.

Klayton asked, "So how much do y'all need to put on your lil' hog festival? I'm feeling generous today, although I don't particularly know why, but perhaps I'd be willing to give a modest donation. Hell, I'm just gonna write it off anyways. Will a few hundred bucks help ya out?

"Sir, at this point we'd accept any and all donations. Giving is a heart condition. Truth be told we grateful for anything we get. But if I can just keep it real wit'cha, a few hundred dollars ain't even enough to buy the seasonings for the meat. We cook upwards of 40,000 pounds of meat alone. Again, that don't include the fix'ins such as fries, slaw, corn on the cobb or drinks. Not to mention we have live entertainment and their bills don't stop just cause they like to play, you feel me?"

During their conversation, Klayton's food had arrived and before he tore into those gizzards as if he hadn't eaten in the spell of a month or better, he took a brief moment to sniff and savor the aroma of the plate set before him. Ol' King took a long hearty whiff of the food. To say he was pleased with the meal would be an understatement. He smiled with every bite, almost to the point where he had to make a conscious effort to keep his mouth closed while chewing. Now, while they weren't exactly Bessie-Mae caliber, they were a close second, even if not for the mere fact that they were a rare find. Surely this meal was working its way through him in more ways than one. Klayton was confident his flirtatious moment with nostalgia had something to do with prompting his generosity. He had just begun to guzzle down the ice-cold beer when Trey mentioned the amount of meat they cooked during the festival and almost choked, but managed to exclaim,

"Good Lord! 40,000 pounds of pork! It's no wonder why y'all dying from heart disease, hypertension and diabetes. Whaddya feeding, a village?" Another patron who was also seated at the bar chimed in, "You'd be surprised how fast you can blow through 40,000 pounds of hog when you feeding hungry people that come from all over just to break bread together." The man speaking was Big Earl Heizleburg, also known as one of the event's pit masters. He continued, "Besides, it's never been just about the food. No one ever leaves hungry or without feeling good about themselves."

"Or without having a good time!" Sadie interjected.

Big Earl smiled and continued, "You tell him, Sadie! It's really about the people, brother. Do you realize that some of these folks plan their vacation time around this event every year? I know this might not mean anything to you and you think we're just a bunch of nobodies in a God-forsaken hell hole, eating our way to our graves, but we matter. If to no one else but each other, everybody matters in this *village*."

It was hard to tell just why Klayton had gone completely silent after Big Earl had spoken. Maybe he was in awe of how large of an individual this was. Big Earl had earned his name. He was a behemoth of a man at 6'8", 330 lbs. He was chiseled, arms like tree trunks, bald and had a beard 12 inches long. He was quite the specimen and looked very intimidating, but the truth of the matter was, he was an assistant pastor overseeing the children's ministry at the local church. Or maybe Klayton was just having a 'come to Jesus' moment. Who knows? He just knew he'd spent enough time here. Much more than he'd anticipated and he was ready to go. Besides, he still needed answers to the real questions of the day, and he was well over an hour and a half away from his destination.

As he stood up to leave, he looked around like he was taking it all in and then he pulled out two crisp $100.00 bills from his pocket and gently placed them on the bar with a double tap. His eyes met Sadie's and he nodded as he said, "Ma'am, thank ya and please give my compliments to the cook. Those were the best gizzards I've had in a very long time."

Sadie rendered a half-smirk, half-smile and said, "Yeah, her mama would be real proud, I'll let her know."

Trey extended his hand to shake Klayton's and said something that would stick with him for a very long time. "Mr., it's been real having you here in our little town. Ordinarily I'd extend an invitation for you to come back and see us sometime, but if you don't even believe that God would come here in the first place, then my offer to you would really be kinda silly, na wouldn't it? You know my daddy used to say, you can run from a lot of things, and a lot of people, but you can't run from who you are. But that's only if you know. I know something's on you, 'cause people like you don't run from the life they have to come here. Most people that come here *wanna* be here. I pray you find peace on your journey. On behalf of the good citizens of Greensville County, we wish you safe travels. Be blessed na, sir."

Klayton found himself stammering in an attempt to apologize for the 'God not coming here' comment. He felt a lump in his throat the size of a Texas bullfrog. But he was abruptly cut off by Trey saying,

"What's understood don't need to be discussed." Trey sat on a stool at the bar and swiveled around with his back facing Klayton and scrolled through his phone. There was no more mention of a donation of any kind from anyone. As he headed towards the front door, Ol' King was feeling so bad about what he had said, he thought offering any money at this point would just add insult to injury. Or maybe he never intended to give them a dime at all. Who knows? He wondered if there was any truth to his comment, about God not caring about the people of Emporia. But if they were willing to wait on God to provide, then who was he to interfere with their faith? Let 'em wait!

The citizens of Emporia, specifically the ones in the diner at the time, never believed for one second that Klayton Kincheloe was the answer to their prayers. Certainly, God would've chosen to send a more decent person to bless them if He was going to do it in that manner. On the other hand, they didn't want to box God in on how He chose to bless them. They knew if God spoke through an ass to Balaam, He could certainly bless them through the one that just left their diner. See, what they had come to learn about faith is that you've got to have it first, then you got to put it to work even when it doesn't look or feel like things are working in your favor. It's easy for you to say you've got it, but walking like you've got it, now that's another story altogether! They weren't the type of people to let the size of their circumstances appear to be bigger than the God they served. They knew a thing or two about adversity. But they also knew God showed up every time they faced it.

Klayton was back on the road and found

himself consumed with thoughts of his partially pleasant but mostly unusual encounter at the diner. He knew that he was having other DNA tests done, but for some reason he felt conflicted about his feelings towards people of color. How could this one conversation have such an effect on his spirit, to make him question one of his strongest-held beliefs?

He wondered, could he have been wrong about something he'd considered a fundamental truth all this time?

He started to think that just maybe his life of privilege and excess could be a contributing factor as to why the Pork Festival in Emporia was facing extinction. It wasn't like there wasn't enough money to go around in this world. Klayton had more than he would be able to spend in five lifetimes. But the greed of the wealthy and their unwillingness to share left honest, hard-working folks with little to nothing. Moderation is an idealistic term that is only applicable to the working class.

Was he one of those people? Of course, he was. Was this simply a case of the haves and the have nots? Of course, it is! But more importantly, why was he ok with being a racist? The people at the diner seemed like decent enough people. Even after his insensitive remarks, they remained dignified. How did he come to despise such people, simply because of their skin color? Afterall, he didn't even know them.

And then it hit him like a bolt of lightning. Some might even call it an epiphany. The only reason he felt this way was because he was *taught t*o do so. His feelings weren't even *his* own. His thoughts had conformed to that of other influences in his life. The teachings of his father and grandfather came barging to the forefront of his mind. He realized he had very little interaction with anyone that was a different color than he was. Well, except for Bessie-Mae's boys. They were just kids back then and it didn't even matter to them. And as most kids do, they got along and played together just fine; and then the adults got involved.

But as an adult, that singular encounter at the diner was it. Klayton was growing tired of trying to make sense of everything. He just wanted things to go back to the way they were. He missed Ms. Abigail dearly. He missed his friends, or who he thought were his friends. This was just all a big misunderstanding and as soon as his DNA results came back, they'd understand. All would be forgiven and things would be set right again. Little did he know, things would never, ever go back to the way they used to be.

CHAPTER 5
Denial Is Deadly

King finally arrived at his mother's house and the inquisition began. It wasn't an easy line of questioning, but he needed answers. He wanted to know if his parents had been unfaithful to one another. He wanted to know how much richer he could become after he sued the company for screwing up his DNA information, or for the breach in security that led to his information being compromised. He wanted to know their ancestral history and if they'd be willing to take a test to clear up some things as well. That's where he ran into a stone wall. Klayton insisted, and then attempted to demand, that his parents take a DNA test with him.

His mother Miriam attempted to quell his concerns.

"Now honey, you're getting all worked up over nothing. You said yourself there had to be some logical explanation for this. And I'm sure there is. Why, that company clearly made a dreadful mistake. But I don't have any issue with taking a test."

Klayton replied, "Thank you Mama, I rightly appreciate it. Daddy, what about you? Surely, you'd be willing to take a test so I can set things right with the boys of the PMG as well as Abigail, wouldn't you?

"Actually, I'm not the least bit interested in participating in any of that foolishness!" The conviction of Avril's denial came as a shock to Klayton, "Especially for the likes of that silly little group of yours with them misfits or that girl! You should've broken up with her years ago, when me and her daddy stopped doing business together."

Klayton just barely managed to keep his temper in check, "*That girl* is slated to be your daughter-in-law! Or have you forgotten? And I don't see what your business relationship with her father has to do with us anyway! But I'm interested to hear why are you so against taking a test. Is there something you'd like to share?"

By this time, Avril was standing. His patience had worn thin with his son and he felt the need to make his position on the topic explicitly clear. "As a matter of fact there is something I'd like to share with you, my sentiments about this whole bag of foolishness! Listen closely. I do not now, nor have I ever, believed in those stupid tests! You don't know what they're putting in those things to yield the results they desire. Are you in the lab with them when they're processing your little vial of spit? No, you're not! Furthermore, I don't need anyone trying to convince me of *their* findings about who they say I am. I know exactly who I am and I know the stock that courses through my veins! Why, if you were to cut me open right now, I'd bleed pure, White American blood!" Avril was clearly done with entertaining his son's inquiries and the conversation as a whole. "I certainly hope that there's more to you beckoning me here than what's been requested of me so far. I am a terribly busy man, Klayton. I run more than a boys club, The insult wasn't even veiled, "and perhaps if you were more focused on the same, instead of running up behind your *fiancée* and those idiots you call friends, you'd be getting somewhere with your life. I have had my fill of this hokum! In fact, more than enough for one day."

Klayton was reeling from the blow his father had just dealt, but he was not about to concede so easily this time without saying how he felt. "Well Daddy, you never were one to mince words now, were ya? Regardless of anyone's thoughts or feelings. Well, I won't take up any more of your precious time. Forgive me for thinking that this time might've been different from any other when I came to you with a problem. What's understood don't need to be discussed, right Daddy?"

Miriam remained mostly silent during the exchange between the two men, with the exception of the tinkling noise her spoon made when stirring and hitting the side of the China teacup she held between nervous hands.

Avril inched towards the exit and managed to utter, "I'll be in Amsterdam for a few days, starting tomorrow. If either of you need to reach me for matters of substance, you know how."

Klayton stood looking out of the window with his back to his father, his hands clasped behind his back. Avril lovingly kissed Miriam on the cheek, gave Klayton one final glare, and let himself out. The silence was a bit awkward but was soon broken by Miriam, asking Klayton if he would like to join her in the parlor for a cup of tea. He declined respectfully, telling his mother he was just dog tired and needed to lie down for a spell.

Truthfully, he was no less confused as he had been before he arrived. Klayton asked if it would be alright with her if he stayed for a few days until he was able to sort things out. He was still far too discombobulated to face anyone in his hometown right now.

"Now, don't be silly hon, you know this is and always has been your home. Stay as long as you'd like. I do believe there are still some clothes of yours in the armoire in your room." It was exactly what Klayton needed to hear.

"Thank you, Mama…Why was the old man so rattled? It's been a long time since I've seen that side of him. Something ain't right."

Miriam looked at her only son and tenderly smiled, "Now, who knows? Your Daddy is your Daddy and certain things about him aren't ever going to change. Being bull-headed is one of those things. Give him some time, he'll come around.

You'll be talking to one another again before it's anybody's business. Get some rest, Love you son."

"Love you too Mama."

A few days had turned into several weeks and then some. During that time, Klayton remained in an exile of his own making. He was a steaming, hot mess! He had gotten the results back from five different DNA agencies and they all yielded the same results. He made several attempts to speak with Ms. Abigail, but to no avail. He eventually got the picture, cause each time he called her he could hear Clete's voice in the background or vice-versa when he called Clete's phone.

Any question he still had on the matter was answered the day he called Abigail, only to have Clete answer her phone, mistaking it for his own.

"Hello?" It was Clete's voice.

Klayton quickly gathered himself, "Clete?"

"Yeah, this is him, who's this?"

"Who's this? Oh, you don't recognize my voice now? I ain't been gone that damn long! I'll tell you who this is; this is your employer...better yet, your former employer! You are so fired Cletus Farmbrooke! What the hell are you doing answering my fianceé's phone?"

"Your fiancée? Oh my, she didn't tell you, huh?"

"Tell me what?"

Clete hollered to someone nearby, "Sweet Peaches, you didn't tell him, huh?"

"Sweet Peaches? Who the hell are you calling Sweet Peaches?" Klayton could feel the fervent heat of betrayal raging inside of him like an impending volcanic eruption.

Abigail's unmistakable voice could be heard faintly, exclaiming,

"Tell who what, sugar plumb?"

Clete responded, "Honey, it's you-know-who," then turned his attention back to Klayton, "Listen here, *brother* notice I didn't say *my* brother, I can never use that term in reference to you again, but seeing as how you are one of them now, I just thought I'd try to keep it politically correct. I know things have been a little rough for you lately, so here's a tidbit to brighten your day, given yours and the little lady's history and all. See, we got a sweet deal on some new iPhones." Well, that wasn't quite the turn Klayton was expecting the conversation to take.

"We bought two of 'em at the same time, and wit 'em being identical and all, well that's how the mix-up came about when you called. Now, because we're such loyal customers, obviously something which you know nothing about, they're gonna throw in an extra line and my little Peach here got to thinking, being the sentimental soul that she is, who'd be better to offer it to than King? She's still a little torn up over the whole ordeal you put her through, but we're working through it."

Klayton was beyond apoplectic at this point, "Little lady! Wait a damn minute! First of all, don't call me brother! You ain't no brother of mine and for that matter, don't call me King either! That address is reserved strictly for my friends, which clearly you ain't! Extra phone line? What in the hell are you talking about? Clearly you have lost your ever-loving mind!"

Clete wasn't phased in the slightest, "Au contraire mon frère. Who but a friend would throw you an extra line? I could've offered it to any one of the boys of my beloved PMG. I think that gesture alone speaks for itself."

"YOUR PMG??? Your PMG?? That is MY group, Cletus Farmbrooke! And don't you ever forget it!! And I told you not to call me brother! We watched that episode of The Simpsons together, but it sure don't make you fluent in French! Na put Abigail on the phone you sneaky, slimy, slithery som'bitch!"

Clete replied with a mocking tone in his voice, "Na see here, we was trying to do something good and once again you done went off and messed it up. She's upset now and don't feel much like communicating. Can you blame her? Oh, and by the way, we've decided we're keeping the ring. It saves me the trouble and money of pickin' out another one. And by the other way, I respectfully decline your offer to terminate my employment; I quit! Bye, dummy!"

Clete hung up the phone swiftly, leaving Klayton in a state of utter disappointment and total confusement. I know what the right word is but, I like to say confusement cause it's just a bit more messy than your average confusion.

He stood there for a minute with his mouth wide open. He didn't believe what he just heard. He couldn't believe he was losing everything he thought he loved all at once. There was that word again. He loved being White. He loved the PMG.

And he was pretty sure he loved Ms. Abigail. Where did it end? It had become painfully clear that Clete's dream and his poorly kept secret of wanting to live Klayton's life had now become reality. While Klayton's reality had become his own personal nightmare, and all at his own expense.

It was also while staying with his mother, Klayton received the horrific news that my nephew, his father, Avril Kincheloe, committed suicide while away on business in Amsterdam. Klayton could have just died himself. He was consumed with grief. He stayed in his room for the better part of three days without so much as uttering a single word to his mother or eating anything. While no one could've predicted when something like this might have happened, it really came as no shock to any of us. Avril was under a tremendous amount of pressure and debt.

King felt as though the world as he knew it was crumbling around him. Everything he held dear was slipping away from his grasp. He loved his father and he wished that the last interaction they shared could've ended more pleasantly. He felt ashamed for silently cursing the man who had raised him. He wondered if he somehow played a part in his father doing this with all of his bantering and demanding answers. He desperately wanted nothing more than his father's approval and tried to pattern his life after Avril's. Especially when it came to business.

Regardless of how bad he felt, the truth of the matter was there was nothing he could do to change it now. On top of everything that happened he still had to come to grips with the possibility that he could be Black or part Black or had "Black blood" or whatever he was now. He struggled with more than acceptance. He was fighting against the very things he had taken for granted his entire life. His built-in belief system and things just being the way they were.

His mother knocked on his bedroom door bright and early one morning in a desperate attempt to convince him to accompany her on an outing to the farmer's market. She was hopeful that he'd go with her, but not surprised when he refused. She informed him that she had made breakfast and placed his portion in the oven to keep warm. She was adamant that he eats it before she returned and reminded him of all the love and labor that she put into making it while thinking of him. She had no problem using motherly guilt to get him to eat something.

At that point, he just wanted to get her away from his door and get her moving on her way. So, he agreed to eat the breakfast she had made for him. Not a full minute later he heard her pick up her keys and leave out the front door. He waited while the sound of her little sports car faded into the distance and only then did he emerge from his room. He ventured into the kitchen where he opened the warming drawer of the oven and retrieved the food waiting for him.

He loved his mother's cooking and after days of not eating, suddenly found himself with a ferocious appetite. Two pieces of country bacon, scrambled eggs with cheddar cheese, a hefty mound of grits with two pats of butter almost completely melted on top. Two slices of wheat toast glazed with her own home-made, honey-pecan, marmalade spiced jam. He ate heartily and wanted so badly to go to sleep afterwards. Yes, he had acquired the 'itis.' For those of you that's unfamiliar with what the itis is, it's what'cha get after eating and usually eating too much.

It's when your eyelids feel like they're made from cast iron. But instead of heading back to his bed, he found himself venturing toward the study where his father used to spend a lot of time. He didn't particularly want to go into the study for fear of becoming emotional. However, he felt drawn there. Like something was calling him. But he didn't know what. He stood outside the door momentarily, debating whether to go in before pushing the door wide open with one arm.

Once inside, he walked around the huge oak desk, dragging a finger along the top of it, as if he were inspecting for dust. He stopped and sat in the large chair behind the desk and looked around the entire room slowly, surveying all the details: the books on the shelves; the size of the windows and the amount of light they allowed in; the crown molding; the Tiffany-style lamps on the end tables; the hand-sculpted, ivory chess pieces from Kenya; and the large leather chairs he loved to sit in. His father would sit in one of those chairs, sipping brandy and going over figures while little Klayton sat in the other.

Every item seemed to be important now. The span of about thirty minutes had passed before he forced himself up out of the comfortable chair. As he stood, stretched and yawned he noticed a piece of paper on the floor underneath the center of the desk. He had to get down on all fours to fit himself under the desk and reach the crumpled-up piece of paper. Crawling around on the floor was not a scenario Klayton found himself in very often and he gave a slight chuckle at the oddity of it all. As he pulled himself back to regain his footing, one of his hands met with a spot in the floor that almost seemed to give way. He pressed a little harder with the heel of his hand and sure enough, it felt as if the spot buckled a bit. Well, now his curiosity had gotten the best of him.

The desk sat on top of a huge oriental area rug, and moving the desk to roll back the rug would be no easy feat. But Klayton was up to the challenge. He pushed against one end of the huge, heavy oak desk and it squeaked to the left, barely moving a couple of inches. This was going to take him all night. He thought it might've been a little bit easier seeing how it was on the carpet. So much for wishful thinking. He took frequent breaks in between moving the desk a few inches at a time.

He finally got the corner of the desk moved far enough to roll the rug back. It exposed the soft spot where, much to his surprise he found a small door, almost like a trap door or an escape hatch, built right into the floor. It was made of the same hardwood material as the flooring, with a ring for a handle that was inlaid into the top of it. There was no keyhole or lock to keep prying eyes out, so Klayton went ahead and opened it without a second thought.

Sitting inside a shallow compartment were several manila envelopes, stuffed to the gills with loose pieces of paper. He grabbed a stack of the envelopes and headed to one of the leather chairs that had been pushed aside, up against the wall, out of the way of his activity. There was no writing on the outside of any of them. He opened the first envelope and saw several pictures of people he didn't recognize. He had no idea who any of these people were but found it curious that all of the people were Black, except for a few young White children scattered throughout.

While most of the pictures seemed to be very old, printed in black and white, it was not difficult to see there were various shades of Black represented. No two or three of the men and women he saw appeared to be the same shade. The photos were mostly taken in front of very old, dilapidated houses. The White children were being held by the Blacks and for the life of him, he could not make a guess as to why. There were a few other photos at the bottom of the pile depicting White men seated in front of fair-skinned women that stood behind them. The ladies' skin tones were difficult to distinguish. Klayton kept quietly asking himself, "*Who were these people?*" And even more puzzling, "*What are these pictures doing here...and why were they hidden?*"

CHAPTER 6
Looks Are Deceiving

After sifting and sorting for the better part of an hour, Klayton had determined that there were several photos that appeared to be from a few different eras. He opened the next envelope and there were birth and death certificates. There were census records, marriage and divorce decrees. There was even a ledger with hand-written notes and references of who was who and connecting the dots, giving just a little more detail. On one of the birth certificates was the name *Pervis T. Kincheloe.* Klayton's grandfather. Truth of the matter was,

Pervis himself was mixed-race. At this moment, Klayton realized that race mixing went back further than the documents he had just discovered. This was just the tip of the iceberg. Not only was this a part of America's culture it was also it's History. This revelation alone would have jarred Klayton to his very core but there was so much more.

Pervis had fathered three other children besides Avril with his colored mistress across town, Coralene Patterson. Avril was just the one he decided was worth claiming publicly. He had two other sons and a daughter. Pervis II, Walter Lee and Corliss Maebelle. The children were all mixed-race, as Pervis was, but Avril was light enough to pass for White, even though he knew the truth. Pervis was too ashamed to let it be known that he had fathered children that weren't *"pure"*. Avril was the only child that could pass for White with no question because he had a different mother altogether; Gretchen Kincheloe, who was Caucasian.

During those times it was commonplace for men that were children of slave owners to have multiple families, even if they were of different races.

It was still unacceptable, however, to claim or to publicize that you had colored children. Coralene had given their son Pervis' name as an insurance policy to give her leverage if she ever needed something and he was less than cooperative. She knew he was much too powerful of a man to try to blackmail. She really did it just to spite him. He had been absent when the boy was born and stayed away for nearly two years before returning. Upon his return he was outraged to learn what Coralene had done. This was their third child together and Coralene was fed up with his foolishness.

The children never knew he was their birth father, and after some convincing, she agreed to give the other children a different last name. Pervis fussed and cussed and made all types of threats, but Coralene wouldn't budge on changing Pervis II's name. While she wasn't afraid of him, she did believe he was more than capable of making life uncomfortable for her children.

She didn't want to inflict any unnecessary suffering upon her kids for something they had nothing to do with. Lord knows they would receive their fair share of suffering simply due to the color of their skin without any influence from Pervis. She was bitter because Pervis had abandoned them and was absent for yet another birth. He had forsaken them for his *real* family; therefore, she took matters into her own hands.

Pervis hadn't been present for any of their children's births, but this little feat of hers really rubbed him the wrong way and he never came back around her or their children again.

Pervis intended to have the birth certificate changed himself. He felt secure enough with the document in his personal possession and hidden away. But as time went on, he eventually forgot to address the issue altogether. Very few knew of Pervis's other children and those who did dared not breathe a word of it. Pervis was a very rich and powerful man. He had a way of getting things handled while maintaining his distance from unfortunate events. He was never once named as a suspect or even a person of interest in several calamitous happenings throughout Danville. Everyone knew, but they were all complicit not to mention scared.

While he did not flaunt his mistress and their children, he had very strong convictions about a man taking care of his own. The Bible said that a man who did not provide for those of his own household was worse than an infidel. He vehemently believed that, even if they did live in separate houses. He knew that God had blessed him with more than enough to afford to take care of the lives he had a hand in helping to create. He provided a home for them and always made sure Coralene had enough money to get whatever they needed. He felt responsible for what happened to them. That's why he made sure Pervis II got the job at the railroad station. It was also why he had the managers refer to him as "Boss Man" whenever he made an appearance. There was no need to raise suspicion by using his real name.

Klayton sat motionless on the floor in disbelief from what he just discovered. These were family photos. He thought to himself, *"That's why Daddy did it. He knew all along! He'd rather die than to accept the fact and admit we were Black...Wow, unreal!"*

He continued to rifle through the documents, pausing frequently to stare off into the distance as his mind raced with the thought that another part of his life had been completely kept secret from him. He had no idea who he really was anymore. Feelings of confusion, deceit and betrayal welled up within him. As he struggled to hold back tears, his mother walked in.

Miriam spoke as she entered the office, "I see you finally came out and ate, but I really did expect you...to...be asleep by now..." Miriam's voice trailed off in between words as she took in the sight of Klayton sitting on the floor, documents and photographs strewn all around him.

Klayton wasted no time before tearing into her, "Mama, how could you? You knew this whole time and said nothing?" Miriam made a feeble attempt to explain, "Klayton, son, I'm so sorry. It was your daddy he swore me to secrecy. He threatened to take you away from me and never let me see you if I ever spoke a word of it to you. You have to believe me, honey. You know your father was a very powerful and influential man. I believed he'd do it!"

"Aww mama, now you blaming him? I'm so disappointed. I could expect something like this from him, but not from you. I always thought you were different than him. Better even...what was it, the money?"

Miriam fired back, "Now Klayton Jefferson Kincheloe, you mind your tongue young man! You know I never cared about money more than I cared about you! I was willing to walk away from the marriage with nothing but the clothes on my back and the shoes on my feet! I just wanted to be able to see and take care of you and be the best mother I could be to you. But your father couldn't understand that I didn't want anything and felt that at some point I'd tell you the truth. He was right you know. I planned on telling you, but he had that leachy bastard Herbert Strausburg, his attorney, draw up some papers and said if I didn't sign them, I'd never see you again. I mean, what was I supposed to do? He kept talking about his friends who were judges and all the politicians and police commissioners he had on his payroll. He was more than capable."

"I mean, I was scared to death that he'd go through with it. He threw all the money and properties in as some sort of insurance to himself, I guess. I didn't ask for any of it, mind you. I just wanted to be able to see my baby. You believe me don't you son?"

"You know Mama, I really don't know what to believe at this point or who, for that matter. I've gotta get outta here and clear my head. I need some fresh air!" Klayton stormed past his mother, leaving her standing there with all the proof.

Miriam heard the front door slam with such force that she was sure it had come clear off the hinges and was laying in the middle of the floor. She also felt as though someone had kicked her dead square in the chest. Her heart was hurting, and she could barely breathe. She managed to walk slowly to the kitchen to get a glass of water, which helped a little, but only a little.

Klayton was torn between emotions of confusion, fury, and utter sadness. He couldn't believe that he was in such a predicament. He wanted to disappear, but to where? There was no escape for him.

The words he had heard from the young man in the diner several weeks earlier rang in his head, as though the young man were standing right next to him, whispering them in his ear. "You can run from a lot of things and a lot of people, but you can't run from who you are."

The words kept looping over and over again in his mind and for the life of him, he couldn't make them stop. He was certain he was losing his mind. He had no idea of where he was going. He was just driving. He didn't know what direction he was driving in. He just drove. He didn't even care at that point. He just wanted his mind and his spirit to be on one accord-- which was peace.

After driving for about an hour or so, he pulled off the road into a parking lot. He had no idea of where he was. He sat in the parking lot, leaned over the steering wheel and began sobbing. He no longer questioned God, "Why me?" He simply asked God to make his heart stop hurting. He didn't want to feel this way any longer. He just wanted the pain to go away. In between his whimpers were whispers. Barely audible, yet clearly intelligible, he repeatedly said he was sorry. By this time dusk was upon him, when an amber haze of smoke filled the cabin of his vehicle. He was too exhausted to even notice it. Just when he thought he was done crying, he cried some more until he cried himself clear on to sleep.

Klayton was awakened by the tapping of a ringed finger on the glass of his car window.

Startled and disoriented, he tried to gain his bearings. As his eyes began to focus, the darkness outside the car window told him either it was nighttime, a lunar eclipse was taking place, or he was in for one heck of a storm. He couldn't see anything, but his ears suddenly heard a voice that sounded familiar. "Hey brother, you ok in there? You need some help?"

In his mind, he wondered why he was being called *brother*. That term was a bit of a hot point for him presently. Just as Klayton was collecting himself, he rolled down the window and squinted as he looked up with his hand across his forehead looking like a military salute gone very, wrong.

As the voice was nearing the opening of the window, the shadowy figure leaned over and allowed the sun to expose itself while beginning to snicker, saying, "You have got to be kidding me! Anybody that says God doesn't have a sense of humor obviously don't know Him! What are you doing here? What are you, a census taker now? Coming back to see how many of us are still alive?"

"What you call a sense of humor, I call cruel and unusual punishment!" Klayton recognized Big Earl and felt an unexpected sense of homecoming as he eased into conversation with this man he barely knew.

"Hey, watch it! You're talking about my God now and besides, who says I'm not the one being punished?"

Klayton chuckled, "I didn't know y'all were exclusive, but point taken. I guess there's enough punishment to go around."

Big Earl shot back, "Yeah, well it's clear He isn't a respecter of persons."

"I have no idea of how I wound up coming here. But since I am here, is there someplace we can go and talk? You a preacher, ain't'cha?"

"Yeah, I am and I can think of few hundred reasons how you wound up here. Look I was just heading to the diner to grab something to eat and then come back here. I'm working late tonight at the church. You can come to the diner with me and we can talk there." Earl offered politely.

"Oh God, no, not there! I don't mean it like that, but I can't show my face there again. I didn't leave the best impression, I'm sure."

"Well, to be totally honest, no, you didn't, but we are very forgiving people. I didn't hear anybody say one bad thing about you while you were there.

But I'm sure if they did, it would be more than one thing. And after you left, well, that's something different altogether and just because I didn't hear it, don't mean they didn't say it..." Big Earl sounded like he could go on forever. But Klayton had heard enough and quickly cut him off with,

"Alright, alright, I get it! I get it! But in all seriousness, I can't show up back there, not just yet anyway. Man, those chicken gizzards sure was good eating though. I don't know if they worth-getting-killed-for good, but man they were tasty!" Klayton could feel his mouth watering at the thought.

"I tell you what, I've already placed my order, it just needs to be picked up. I'll put an order in for you on the way there and bring it back. You hang out here for a bit. We can talk over supper, how's that sound?"

"Sounds like my belly will forever be indebted to you! I'll be right here."

Twenty minutes later, Big Earl came pulling back into the lot.

Klayton got out of his car and the two men entered the church through a side door. Once inside, they went to Big Earl's office, said grace and began to eat. While they ate, or *broke bread,* as Big

Earl liked to refer to it, Klayton found himself talking so much it seemed more like a confessional than a conversation. He told the pastor about his upbringing and about his father's passing. He even questioned whether his father would get into Heaven after what he'd done to himself. He talked about his recent findings in his father's study, and how he just felt run down and ragged. He expressed the resentment he held against his father and grandfather for steering him towards hate, instead of letting him figure out who he liked and disliked for himself and for his own reasons. He spoke about how confused and angry he was with the Lord.

He told Earl about how his mother played a part in all the secrecy and deception and how he was feeling about her. He talked about the PMG and Ms. Abigail and Clete and what they did to him and how Ms. Abigail could very well be Mrs. Cletus Farmbrooke by now. Oh, he bared his whole, tired, lil' ol' soul!

Finally, he asked about how he could change for the better. Pastor Earl had an answer for just about everything he threw at him. And what he couldn't answer, they prayed about it. Pastor Earl spoke to him about the importance of forgiveness and the more you did it, the healthier you'd be and the longer you'd live. He thought it was important for him to have peace in knowing his father was with God.

He also told him that his money meant nothing to anyone but himself and he'd find himself with a lot less of it if he continued to use it for manipulative and destructive purposes. He couldn't quite remember where he had heard this quote from but he knew he was particularly fond of it and used it every time an opportunity presented itself for him to do so. He told Klayton, "No one cares how much you know until they know how much you care." Klayton found this to be rather profound and inspiring. He admired it and thought one day he might be able to quote it to someone that he was helping. Well, Klayton felt like he had talked too much, ate more than he talked, and stayed for much longer than he planned to, but he did feel better. He was just about ready to leave but before doing so he had a favor to ask of Pastor Earl.

"I already know that I ain't a town favorite and that's ok with me, but I do wanna do something for the people of this town. I wanna make a donation to the pork festival. But you can't tell anyone it came from me."

Big Earl raised an eyebrow, "I thought you already did that with the two yards you left on the counter at the diner? For the seasonings remember? I'm just kidding. But where am I supposed to tell people the money came from?"

"I'm not quite sure, but that's your problem. You'll figure something out." Pulling a check out of his back pocket, Klayton added,

"Who do I write this out to?"

"Uhm, I suppose you can write it out to the city of Emporia? The church has an account with the city and if necessary we can endorse it. Shouldn't be problem."

Klayton scribbled his signature at the bottom of the check and handed it to Pastor Earl, who looked at the check in disbelief before replying, "Wow! That's very generous! But I hope you're not trying to buy the people of Emporia's forgiveness because it's not for sale."

Klayton rolled his eyes, "Of course I'm not trying to buy anybody's forgiveness. I'm sure y'all would charge a hell of a lot more than that anyways. But you never did agree that you wouldn't tell 'em it was from me. Can you do that?"

"Yeah, I could, but I'm interested in knowing why? Why are you doing this?"

"You know, I never claimed to be the quintessential Christian, but I do believe that it says somewhere in the Bible, that it's better to give than to receive. And while I may not be the loudest advocate for that theory, I know there's a need. And when ya know better ya supposed to do better. At least that's what my daddy used to tell me. So, I'm trying to do better."

Big Earl flashed a smile that was almost as big as he was, while Klayton managed to produce an awkward smaller one, but a smile nonetheless.

Standing there with a check for $175,000.00 dollars in his hand, Big Earl took a moment to reflect before saying, "Hey, this money is great and we really, really do appreciate it, don't get me wrong, but we still don't have enough volunteers to make this festival move. Unless we can get that sorted, this money isn't goin' anywhere.

"Good Lord, man! Do I have to do everything? Guess it ain't enough that I'm donating my entire life savings to this event, huh?" Klayton took a dramatic pause, "I'll see what I can do. Next, you'll be wanting me to fill in on the grill."

Big Earl replied matter-of-factly, "Life savings, yeah right! Hey, we'll take all the help we can get! By the way, you ever roasted a whole hog before?" "Looka' here, No I have not and I ain't about to either!"

CHAPTER 7
Reconciliation & Redemption

A couple of weeks had passed and during that time Ol' King had done some soul-searching. He patched up things with his mama and even mustered up the courage to return to his own home. He felt he needed a change of scenery; a downsize even. After all, it was just him living in the 6-bedroom, 7 ½ bath, 10,000 sq. foot estate all by his lonesome. And with no immediate plans for a Mrs. Kincheloe on the horizon, he figured it was time for something a little different.

He started to realize that change could be a good thing... but it was also evolution. And evolution was inevitable. It's going to happen whether you want it to or not. There are some things that are just out of your control. Either you go right, or get left. Plain and simple.

While back in Danville, he'd made a stop at his old buddy Clete's house. He left before the police were called, but not before giving Clete and his 'little lady' both a piece of his mind and a few choice words. I bet that was quite the sight. He even managed to get back his hefty engagement ring from Ms. Abigail. He was a cheap son-of-a-gun! And he sure wasn't gonna let the likes of Clete Farmbrooke get out of having to pay for his own engagement ring. Now, he could have the girl, but he wasn't getting both!

During his time away, Klayton decided to become more actively invested in the companies and businesses that brought him exorbitant wealth. He drew up an executive order that was addressed to all the presidents of his companies. The order stated that they must cease any and all discriminatory practices that held any employee back from seeking advancement, solely based on the color of his/her skin, sexual orientation, religious creed, ethnicity, age or any of the other things that they said they didn't discriminate against in the hiring process, but really did. He, in his old Klayton "King" Kincheloe way, let them know, in no uncertain terms that this was the dawn of a new era and there was a new way of doing business.

He had no idea what he'd actually do if they weren't compliant. He just knew he had to warn them that there would be consequences for being disobedient. And not so much from his hand, but from the hand of his Father. His Heavenly Father, who he had gotten reacquainted with in recent times. He had even decided to get baptized by none other than Pastor Big Earl Heizelberg himself. Initially, he was a little apprehensive that Big Earl might not bring him back up out of the water quickly enough. But those fears were quickly washed away after he was told and showed how much he was loved by Jesus and the people of the community in the town of Emporia.

For the life of him, he just couldn't understand how he could be accepted as he was and had been for so long. He had the darnedest time trying to wrap his head around the concept that he couldn't afford to pay for something that had already been paid for. He was used to buying whatever he wanted; it just seemed unfathomable to him that he didn't have enough money to afford *this* gift. He knew he hadn't been a good person, employer, friend, fiancée or even neighbor. He soon realized the difference between tolerating people, and actually accepting them and just loving them as people. He also realized that he hadn't been loving people the way God loved him, which was unconditionally which included a time when he was not very lovable. Ultimately, he came to the realization he simply needed to give people a chance and get to know them.

At any rate, he was growing. Not just as a man, but as a part of the human race, which he was proud to be a part of and as far as he was concerned today, was the only race that mattered.

He found himself sitting on a small park bench, listening to great music fill the air along with the smell of award-worthy barbeque. There were people all over the place. Some were dancing and singing along with the songs the band was playing. Most of them were chowing down on delicious food and enjoying great conversations.

They mattered...if to no one else but each other. He saw that clearly now.

He was thankful to be in the position he was in; to be blessed enough to bless others including the people of Emporia and help them pull off their annual pork festival. From what he could tell, it appeared to be a success. He, like his father, knew some important people that owed him a few favors. So, he called one in and was able to round up enough "volunteers" to help out. Turned out, it wasn't so bad knowing the warden of Wallens Ridge State Prison and having him owe you a favor or two.

The way Klayton looked at it, he created an opportunity for these "volunteer" inmates to be around some level of normalcy and enjoy some good food and music while providing a needed service. They got to create new memories in a positive environment, giving them something to talk about for some time to come. For the ones that were fortunate enough to have a release date, well, it'd give them something to look forward to. His sentiments, not mine. I am in no way promoting or endorsing modern day prison slave labor. Just bear in mind, that Rome wasn't built in a day. Lord knows the boy still needs work.

While sitting on the bench, another familiar face approached, asking if he could take up some real estate beside him. Klayton responded, "Last I checked, Emporia was in the US and this is still a free country."

Trey stood near the bench where Klayton was seated, "Last I checked, wasn't nothing free in this country but the word, but even that depends on where you go nowadays. What's up man? Just couldn't stay away, could you? What'cha doing back here? Making sure God forgot about us? I know you paid for this too! Thank you."

"I don't know what makes you think that? Besides I ain't the only person with money. Actually, I thought I'd just stop by to see how things were going before heading out to see my mother and look at a few properties. And since I was here, figured I'd pick up a rib or two, maybe a pulled pork sammich while I'm at it."

Klayton had obviously made a scene worth remembering when he'd dined on those gizzards months ago. Trey remembered and seized the opportunity. "A sammich huh? Well, unfortunately we don't have your favorite on the menu today; barbeque chitterlings. I hope you ain't too disappointed!" This was Trey's way of being humorous, at least to himself.

"Not at all! Not at all, Pervis."

Trey cut his chuckle short and snapped his head around quickly, "What you call me?" "Pervis the third, right? Pervis Treyford Kincheloe III. Trey is short for Treyford, right?"

Trey responded hesitantly, "Hey, man...who are you? And how you know my name?"

"Well, let's just say we have more in common than either one of us might care to have or ever knew we had."

"Yeah alright I hear you, but that still don't answer my questions...who the hell are you and how do you know my name?"

Klayton could see that he hadn't handled this conversation as delicately as he'd imagined and tried to offer a soothing, "Calm down, calm down."

"My guy, don't be telling me to calm down! I don't know you and you don't know me, but you come up in here calling me by my government name like you got some business with me. Na, this the last time I'm gon' ask you who the f--..."

Klayton interrupted him, "Listen...listen, listen to me...we're cousins, alright?" Any further attempt at subdued mystery went out the window.

"Cousins? Man, get the hell outta here with that!" Trey was obviously not buying it.

"As strange as it may sound...we are. Can't tell you I'm ecstatic about it myself, but I did one of them DNA tests, well, several of 'em actually, and found some other documentation that led me to discover that my grand-daddy, Pervis Treyford Kincheloe the first, is your grand-daddy as well. How else would I know who you are and what your entire *government* name is and all that other good stuff? Trey stood there with a stern look on his face, appearing to absorb the shock of a heavy blow.

"My daddy and your daddy are brothers, but with different mothers. We also have an aunt and uncle in common. Your daddy ever tell you anything about his upbringing? Like, who his parents were? Where he was from? Whether he had any siblings?" Klayton wasn't sure how he had expected this conversation to go, but Trey was turning out to be a hard nut to crack.

"Hey man, I ain't telling you shit about me, my daddy, or none of my people. For all I know, you could be working for the feds, or the friends of the court, or you might even be a sex trafficker! Bruh, I don't know you!"

Klayton was doing his best to keep cool. This was undoubtedly an unusual situation for both of them. "Look-a here, I don't work for no damn feds, and to the contrary, a few of 'em work for me, but that's neither here nor there. As far as the friends of the court, that's quite unlikely. I don't think they send people out after ya, they just garnish your wages, if you working. Besides, do you owe child support? Are you even working?"

"Yes! I am working and man I don't even got no damn kids!" Trey responded, throwing his arms into the air.

"Well you mentioned'em and that you know of..."

"Here you go with that bullsh--!"

Klayton quickly interjected, "Shhhh, relax! I represent none of those agencies. Sex trafficking? Are you kidding me? What are you, like, 12?"

Trey was still shaking his head in disbelief, "Don't act like that stuff don't be happening for real! What are you really here for, man?"

"I already said why I'm here. Now you can be in denial if you want to, like I was, that's up to you. I didn't come here to *convince* you that we're related. Hell, I had reservations about whether I should say anything at all. Just thought you might've been interested. Besides, once I decided to tell you, don't you think that's the decent thing to do? Lord knows I wouldn't want anybody to have to go through what I went through just to find out the truth which somebody could've just shared with me all along. I got documentation that'll support what I'm telling you. Just to put your mind at ease and lower your suspicion of who I am or what I want. Believe me, besides for maybe a few cooking lessons, there's nothing that I want from ya." Klayton felt like he was saying too much and not enough all at the same time.

"Trust me, I've been on the receiving end of what you're tasting now but believe me when I tell you it's a far cry from the spread y'all got here today. But by the grace of God I've been digesting it little by little each day."

"Yeah, well mighty funny you back here outta nowhere. What's the matter? Let me guess, your people disowned you? Found out you was really a brother and now they don't wanna have nothing to do with your ass, huh? Your girl probably left you too!

"My, my aren't you the insightful one? You know I remember you being a lot more hospitable the last time I was here. Or is it that you were just too busy admiring my *Unicorn Rolly*? They say if you stick around long enough, people start to show their true colors, and they were right. But anyway, you are correct in every assessment you've made about me. But don't go thinking you can judge me, 'cause that job's already been taken. Besides, like I said, I didn't come here to *convince* you of anything, just to share some information with you. The proof is in the pudding. I actually thought you might appreciate some history and education about yourself." Klayton took a long, deep breath to help calm himself before continuing.

"You know, someone once told me that you can run from a lot of people and a lot of things, but you can't run from who you really are. And quite frankly, I'm just tired of running. So, if you don't mind, I'm just gon' continue to sit here for a spell, listen to some good music, enjoy some good food and then be on my merry old way. Now, you're more than welcome to join me if you like, but it's up to you 'cause either way, I'm just too tired to really give a shit! If you do stay, just be quiet so I can hear the music in peace, 'cause if I can just keep it real with you, cuz, your voice is quite annoying."

Trey stood there for what seemed like an eternity but was really no more than about ten seconds. He rubbed both of his hands up and down on the thighs of his pants as if he were drying them off, shaking his head from side to side. He sighed heavily before sitting himself down and settling in next to his newfound kinfolk.

The End

Made in the USA
Columbia, SC
25 May 2023